Carlos Guillermo Wilson

SHORT STORIES BY CUBENA

Translation, Introduction and Notes
by
IAN ISIDORE SMART

Afro-Hispanic Institute

Washington, D.C.

PERMISSIONS

The Introduction was first published as "Big Rage and Big Romance: Discovering a New Panamanian Writer," by Ian I. Smart, in *Caribbean Review*, Florida International University, 8, No. 3. Reprinted with permission of the editor.

"The Flour Boy," a short story by Cubena, translated by Ian Smart, was first published in *Caribbean Review*, Florida International University, 9, No. 2. Reprinted with permission of the editor.

An English version of "Coal and Milk," translated by Ian I. Smart, first appeared in *Ufahamu*, University of California, Los Angeles, 7, No. 3. Reprinted with permission of the editor.

"The African Grannie," translated by Ian I. Smart, was first published in *Afro-Hispanic Review*, 2, No. 2. Reprinted with permission of the editor.

Library of Congress Catalog Card Number: 86-071821
International Standard Book Number: 0-939423-00-6

Cover design by Ken Smith.

Published and distributed by
AFRO-HISPANIC INSTITUTE
3306 Ross Place, N.W., Washington, DC 20008. (202) 966-7783

TO: Buena Isidra
        and
    Monifa Isidra

ACKNOWLEDGMENTS

The following persons and organizations, among others, have helped me to make this book a reality. For this I am truly grateful.

My friend, Carlos Guillermo Wilson, who allowed me to translate his book.

The Andrew W. Mellon Foundation, which through a grant to the Humanities Division of the College of Liberal Arts, Howard University, gave partial financial support to my work.

The Afro-Hispanic Institute, which has given me constant moral and material support.

My colleagues and students at Howard University as well as my colleagues and friends at the Afro-Hispanic Institute, who continue to be a real source of inspiration.

My wife, who foots all the bills, physical, psychological, and ultimately fiscal.

ESCUDO CUBENA

6

Cubena Coat of Arms

Explanation of the Cubena Crest
that appears on the opposite page.

CUBENA – The Spanish form for KWABENA. Professor Carlos Guillermo Wilson, Ph.D. is of
African origin and was born on a Tuesday.
The TWI-speaking ASHANTI people of
GHANA, AFRICA have the custom of
naming their boy children after the day on
which they were born.

EBEYIYE – A TWI word, meaning: "the future will be
better."

The chain of six links represents the six
principal African groups who were enslaved in the
Americas: the YORUBA, FANTI, ASHANTI, CONGO-
LESE, BANTU, and the DAHOMEAN peoples.

The three stars symbolize Cubena's family's
three homelands: AFRICA–JAMAICA–PANAMA.

The book stands as a symbol of the most
important arm in the battle against intellectual servi-
tude. The tortoise represents the patience and strength
of character which African peoples have had to develop.
The bee, trying to penetrate the hard strong tortoise
shell with its sting, symbolizes the blows, insults and
chains which black people have had to endure with
heroic fortitude.

7

TABLE OF CONTENTS

Introduction*

The most impressive critical appraisal of this young Panamanian's work comes from the pen of one of the elder statesmen in the field of Afro-Hispanic-American literature. The prominent Ecuadorian literary figure, Adalberto Ortiz, author of *Juyungo* (1942), the first of the important black novels emanating from Spanish America, has said in an unpublished review: "In his *Short Stories by Cubena the Black*, in other words stories told by the author himself, Cubena adds a new note to Afro-HispanicAmerican narrative: a kind of black *tremendismo*." Ortiz's words underscore what seems to be the most fundamental trait of Cubena's prose writings, for *tremendismo*, as the name implies, is a literary overindulgence in the horrendous, engaged in for definite artistic ends by certain 20th century Spanish novelists, of whom José Camila Cela is perhaps the best known. Cubena's short stories are indeed a most artistic expression of intense outrage. However, in his poems — which he calls *Pensamientos* (Reflections) — which appeared in print just a few months after the

---

* This was first published as "Big Rage and Big Romance: Discovering a New Panamanian Author," *Caribbean Review*, 8 (Summer 1979), 34-38. Some minor rewording and additions were necessary in order to update the essay.

11

short stories, the bitter recrimination and outrage give way to the tender expression of romantic sentiments.

Cubena's choice of genres is particularly apt. The *Cuentos* (Short Stories) is his first published work. This genre requires the efficient concentration of power, the constant struggle to maintain that fragile balance between intensity and brevity. Cubena's poems (*Pensamientos*), with few exceptions, are also models of intensity and brevity. It is evident to all of us who know Cubena that his personality is shaped precisely by this dynamic dialogue between the forces of brevity and those of intensity.

His prose has the bare factual flavor of a newspaper report, creating an air of authorial detachment with its strongly objective and realistic tone. However, this tone is deceptive: it is merely an artistic device for giving full vent to the immense outrage that wells up in Cubena as he looks deeply at the world around him. His stories are not meant to document faithfully the horrors of this world, but to be expressions of the disgust that these horrors evoke. "Coal and Milk" and "The Family" would make very little sense unless viewed more as metaphor than as fact.

Cubena further adds to the newspaper-report flavor of his prose, by giving a truncated quality to his narrative through the use of the ellipsis. His aim seems to be simply to state the essential facts with a steady, stacatto rhythm. To this end the paragraphs are normally quite short, many consisting of one line. They are like mini explosions preluding the final gigantic explosion of the last paragraph. The following is one of the paragraphs from "Coal and Milk": "When the ceremony in Santa Ana Plaza was over, curses and sobs filled up the most

wretched of the shacks. Every Sunday, every Wednesday . . ." (p. 28). This quote is immediately preceded in
the original text by a six-line paragraph dealing with the
deplorable institution of an additional Wednesday
drawing of the pernicious National Lottery. The ellipsis
at the end of the paragraph quoted above proclaims
the author's deliberate decision to be brief. In fact, he
proceeds directly to a new point, having said all that he
needs and cares to say about the Wednesday drawings.

Cubena's poems are cryptic, many of them expressing
a barbed note of protest. *"Demencia"* (Lunacy) for
example reads:

What is lunacy? Lunacy is:
A small Portuguese mouse
fancying himself
in control of

THREE
 AFRICAN
 ELEPHANTS

And what is super lunacy?
Measly Portugal
taking control of

GUINEA-BISSAU
 MOZAMBIQUE
 ANGOLA[1]

The political satire is excellent in that it focuses accur-
ately on real absurdity. Much of the sickening venom of

[1]*Pensamientos del negro Cubena* (Los Angeles: n.p.,
1977), p. 36. I am responsible for this translation and
for all further translations. Further references to this
work will be given in parentheses in the text.

the short stories is absent, but there remains the same carefully chosen frugality of expression. With the poem *"Definición"* (Definition), relatively simple, structural innovations combine with brevity to create a particularly impressive poetic statement.

    What is a
        1 2
         N
         E
    9 – NEGRO – 3
         R
         O
         6

In Yankeeland
or in Panama?

A time bomb

tic - tac - tic - tac - tic - tac
tik - tak - tik - tak - tik - tak
TIC - TAC - TIC - TAK - TIK - TAK (p. 29)

In "Claudine," one of the love poems, the tone is completely different as the intensity and brevity are put to the service of romantic tenderness.

Sólo quiero vivir
sólo quiero amar
pero sufrir
es mi inmenso mar. (p. 42)

I only want to live
I only want to love
but suffering
is my boundless sea.

Reminiscent of the "Haiku" and the epigrams made popular by the vanguard poets of the twenties, "Clau-

14

dine" achieves a profound expression of beauty through the starkest of expressions, the most frugal use of words.

In a good poem, especially in the short poems that Cubena prefers, every line has to be charged with poetic intensity. Every line has to be a "punch line." In a short story, the reduction of spatio-temporal elements necessitates a strong ending, a punch line. Cubena's short stories show true mastery of the punch line device. Even in his poems this flair for the suspenseful organization of material manifests itself quite impressively. The poem *"Juramento"* (Oath) is the best example of such a technique:

> I am no criminal
> neither black nor mulatto boy child
> do I wish to beget
> I am no criminal
> neither black nor mulatto girl child
> am I going to procreate
> I am no criminal
> no half-Indian boy or girl child either
> I am no criminal.
>
> Wretched albino
> Who are you going to hate? (p. 17)

His voice hoarse and heavy with irony, the poet speaks his condemnation of certain racial attitudes. However, this irony hinges on the knowledge that the poetic persona who so proudly proclaims his supposed racial purity and pulchritude is really just a "Wretched albino," the most odious of all, at the very base of the pyramidal social order. So the full sense of the poem cannot be grasped or even guessed at without the final couplet.

15

Cubena's short stories end with an explosive flash that abruptly elucidates the full sense of the preceeding narative. In "Coal and Milk," the opening work, a poor black woman seems to find a way out of her debasing indigence. Much to the suspicious disapproval of her meddlesome, gossip-mongering neighbors, she acquires two dogs. After six pages, heavy with the menace of impending disaster, the reader is with one swift and brutal stroke made aware of the full nauseating truth: "When Coal and Milk returned to the shack, well before the others awoke, the mother of the ragged little brats would force the dogs to vomit so that she could provide food for her family" (p. 30). It will be difficult to find, in any literature, a more consummately disgusting image. With this punch line Cubena induces in the reader a retching reaction that parallels the dogs' action of *vomitar*. The brutal impression that it leaves on the reader's sensibilities will not be easily effaced.

The punch line of "The Morgue," another story of the collection, almost outdoes that of "Coal and Milk" in its violation of the reader's sensibilities. The two stories have quite similar structures, showing the author's eminently successful use of a suspense that withholds the ultimate explanation until the absolutely final line. Throughout the story strong sentiments of indignation are aroused in the reader, as he is made to witness the viciously and patently unjust working of "Canal Zone Justice." The Indian protagonist and his black companion are but two more victims of this infernal machine that "took possession of the poor Indian's body and soul, 'In perpetuity,' just as it had already done with Panama's sovereignty" (p. 65). In the very last paragraph Cubena fully reveals the depths of degradation to which the Indian had sunk, and for which he has been given an extremely cruel and absurd-

16

ly inappropriate punishment: "One night they caught him red-handed — he habitually had sexual intercourse with the corpses, glassy blue gaze and all" (p. 67).

In "The Degenerate Woman," the last lines fully explain the thread of mystery woven into the eight pages of narrative. The explanation hinges on the main female character's "perverse" preference for her white homosexual lover in the face of her interracial, heterosexual relationship with a black virologist, physician, and general "super-negro." (The virologist is incidentally Cubena's namesake and is obviously his alter ego as well.) The very last lines indirectly but unmistakably reveal Genevieve's — for this is her name — lesbianism: "Two naked bodies, inebriated and burning with erotic passion, locked in a volcanic embrace, and the two women's tongues on two of those organs that so bewitch men" (p. 78).

Not all stories are structured for suspense in so perfect a fashion. In "The Brothel," "Honeymoon," "The Family," and to some extent, in "The Party," the last lines are not the sole key to the full meaning of the respective plots. Nevertheless, they are strong emotional charges, restating with intensity the main message of the story. "The Family," for example, presents the sad history of a mother who finds a macabre solution to the desperate daily problem of physical survival for herself and her six fatherless children. She opts for an early reunion with "Olodumare and the other cheerful ancestors in the Kingdom of the Dead" (p. 101). The extremely cynical and totally disrespectful reaction of the racist society to this tragedy is artfully expressed in these final lines of the story: "On the third from the last page of the morning papers one Tuesday, the first of April, there appeared the following bold headlines:

17

MORE BLACKS DIE, THIS TIME AT HOME AND NOT IN A BARROOM BRAWL" (p. 102).

The themes chosen by Cubena illustrate, for the most part, the more sordid aspects of man's inhumanity to man, or more precisely of the white man's inhumanity to man. For a deeply entrenched, systematic racism is the cause of most of the misery in Cubena's fictional universe. The short stories could be divided into three categories.

To the first category belong those that present odd or psychologically abnormal human behavior. Such behavior results from the pressures exerted on the individual by a racist society. The abnormality of the little black boy of "The Flour Boy," who at night in bed compulsively covers himself with flour, could be placed in this class. "The Brothel" and "The Party," similarly, present patterns of behavior that can be classified as only moderately deviant.

A second group of stories deals with human behavior that most reasonable people would unhesitatingly consider deviant and abominable. Almost everyone would instinctively repudiate the mother's act in "Coal and Milk," considering it disgustingly aberrant. In "The Third Illusion" and in "The Degenerate Woman," homosexuality is the central theme. The implied author thereby appears to have uncritically ascribed degeneracy to all homosexuals — a view that represents, consciously or unconsciously, the application of social sanctions on the basis of theological judgment. In fact, Cubena attempts to elicit the reader's contempt for racism by associating racist values with a preference for "perversion." Genevieve, "The Degenerate Woman" is a case in point. In the case of "The Third Illusion," Nelson the protagonist is accosted by a band of little boys in the street and has the following exchange with them:

> Thief.
> But I'm not black.
> Pothead.
> But I'm not black.
> Faggot.
> But I'm not black. (p. 62)

In "The African Grannie," a faithful old black servant sacrifices her own reputation and her liberty to preserve the supposed honor of her elitist white master's family. However, the white master is himself an "impotent faggot," whose wantonly adulterous wife murders him during a sordid quarrel. Although the Indian in "The Morgue" is punished as a criminal, his behavior belongs more appropriately to this second group.

Pathological, disgusting, and so-called "degenerate" behavior is not always criminal. In the third group of stories, however, the criminal element is introduced. "Honeymoon," for example, presents the case of a white father so incensed with racial hatred that he would rather murder his daughter than see her married to a man who is apparently white but of questionable racial background. In "Carnival Tuesday," three white Yankee men brutally rape and murder a thirteen-year-old black girl. These three villains are clearly meant to be up-to-date versions of the perennial ugly American that has always made his odious presence felt in Panama and on the Canal Zone in particular. They are named symbolically Richard Dixon, Edgar Hooper, and John Pitchell, and are all members of the "Social Club of the Masked Men of Kalifornia, Kalabama and Killinois." The same Canal theme recurs in the poems, and especially in "Gatún" in which a similarly effective play on words established a clear association between the KKK (Ku Klux Klan) and the US presence in Panama. The

poem employs a simple but impressive formal device;
it reads:

```
                  K  K  K
                  r  o  o
We don't want     i  c  l
                  n  a  a
                  g
                  a
```

nor hamburger
nor imperialist $
Teddy the thief
we want JUSTICE (p. 19)

Gatún, as the poet explains in a note, is "an important lake in the Panama Canal."   Sam Wallace the
protagonist of "The Fireman" has dedicated his life to
exterminating "uppity" black people. The ritual suicide
and sacrificial slaughter of "The Family" have already
been discussed, as has the sordid murder in "The African Grannie."

Cubena peoples the fictional world of his short stories
mostly with abnormal beings in varying grades of moral,
psychological and even physical decadence. An over-
view of the structure of his book of poems indicates
some degree of consistency with the view of the world
presented in *Cuentos* (Short Stories). The *Pensamientos* are divided into three parts, the first two of
which are *"Las Americas"* (The Americas), and "Africa." These two parts account for thirty-seven of the
book's forty-six pages and the titles clearly announce
the author's continuing concern with socioeconomic
issues, and, of course, with interracial relations. Furthermore, the section entitled "The Americas" has the
following quote from Montesquieu as an epigraph:

"Injustice done to just one is a threat to all" (p. 7).
More pertinently, the epigraph of "Africa," taken from
Vladimir Hertzog and quoted in English, reads as
follows:

> If we lose our capacity to be
> outraged when we see others
> submitted to atrocities
> then we lose our right to call
> ourselves civilized human beings. (p. 31)

A poem like "Iratus" from the section "The Americas" confirms Cubena's black rage. The title also
bespeaks a touch of erudition for *iratus* is Latin for
angry. It begins: "My first cry in this life / was a protest
against injustice." The persona then proceeds immediately to his central focus, the bitter berating of the
Panamanian nation for stripping descendants of Anglo-
phone West Indians of their Panamanian citizenship.
This action was taken in 1941, the very year of Cubena's birth. The high point of the poem's irony is at-
tained in the following lines:

> and in Gringoland
> they give me
> dignity and citizenship
> what irony! (p. 20.)

So indirectly the United States is poetically indicted.
The poem ends on a note of heavy-handed sarcasm:
"AND THEY COMPLAIN ABOUT SOVERIGNTY?"

In these two sections of the book Cubena's rage er-
rupts in short poems that are like mini volcanoes.
"Cabanga Africana" (African Nostalgia, the word "*Ca-*

21

banga" is a popular Panamanian word of African origin which the poet translates as nostalgia) is but another example:

> You snatched me from my
> DEAR AFRICA
> with a deluge of lashes
> for a handful of coins
> and now a strange culture
> is my sad reality.
> Miserable culprit
> an embrace of death
> is what I long to give you. (p. 11)

Miraculously, however, in the third section of the book hate turns to love. As if aware of this sudden shift and the logical inconsistency it implies, Cubena seems to excuse himself with this quote from Dryden (appearing in a Spanish translation) which he uses as the epigraph: "Love is the noblest weakness of the spirit" (p. 39). This short section is an intimate and extremely lyrical account of the poet's real life experiences. Many of the muses who appear here are recognizable, even by name, to those of us who know Cubena. The poet's erotic adventures transcend racial boundaries as the titles of the poems affirm: "My Argentine Woman," "My Puerto Rican Woman," "My Chicana," "My Jamaican Woman," "Indian Enchantress," "Pretty Mulatto Woman," to mention some. True to the romantic tradition, love redeems the misery of his universe; love holds out some hope.

Cubena, a Panamanian-born resident of Los Angeles, California, has created a literature that is a rich mirror of many influences. The extreme *tremendismo* of his prose bears an obvious relationship to naturalism and its many offshoots. There also appears to be some influence of the Jean-Paul Sartre type of existentialist narrative with its gratuitous preoccupation with nausea. The virulent social protest of a Jorge Icaza could also be a possible source of influence. In a story like "The African Grannie," Cubena appears to be influenced by the stylistic experimentation of the contemporary novel in Latin America and elsewhere. In Cubena's poetry there are many echoes of the various brands of *poesía negrista* (Black poetry) with their stress on social protest themes, and their extensive formal experimentation. The love poems are very similar to the epigrammatic poems made popular by the so-called "new" Latin-American poets of the vanguard epoch.

Black rage turned suddenly to romance in the final section of the *Pensamientos* (published after the *Short Stories*). What began with a bang seemed to peter out to a whimper. However, the final soft tone is unequal to the stridency that predominates in the total work. Indeed, with the publication of Cubena's first novel, *Chombo* (Miami: Universal, 1981) it can be determined that the note of hope through romance sounded in the final pages of *Pensamientos del negro Cubena* is really not a harbinger of a new Cubena, chastened by the torment and rising above it.[2] It was rather the final flicker of a now definitively dead optimism. The *tremendismo* has prevailed. Black Latin-American literature has always existed in its oral form; in its

---

[2]For a more complete analysis of Cubena's works, see Ian I. Smart, *Central American Writers of West Indian Origin: A New Hispanic Literature* (Washington, D.C: Three Continents Press, 1984), especially Ch. 4 "Cubena's West Indian Rage," pp 69-86.

23

written form it has come of age only in this century. Cubena's *tremendismo* is just one of its many manifestations.

TRANSLATOR'S NOTE:

I have used as far as possible conversational Trinidadian English to render the conversational Panamanian Spanish passages. The reason for this is compelling: I am a Trinidadian and the conversational variety of English that I handle best is the one with which I grew up.

And so without my cloth,
shoulders uncovered
to this new doubt

and desert I return,
expecting nothing;
my name burnt out,

a cinder on my shoulder.

Edward Kamau Brathwaite

Coal and Milk

The incessant snivelling of the snotty-nosed, lice-ridden, ragged little urchins was enough to drive one mad. They whined in unison. In a dark, untidy, pestilent corner of the shack their mother, her body aching from her husband's bites and kicks, stooped over a coal-pot warming a little sugar water to soothe the hungry little whiners.

It was always the same ruckus in the drunkard's house: every other week the alcoholic would get home inebriated, pissing his pants and pitilessly beating the poor woman, giving full vent to his cruelty. When he tired of the pugilistic routine, he would violently rip off the unfortunate woman's patched up rags. She would cry out in shame, "the children, the children." But, before she could shriek out the third "the children" the chair, the table, the bed would be sprinkled with semen.

On the frequent occasions when the battered woman fell ill, the eldest daughter was obliged willy-nilly to take her place over the coal-pot and even in the drunkard's bed. The filthy, perpetually starved little ones grew quite accustomed to the vulgar spectacle.

The drunkard's growls had lost their ferocity and the children even reached the point of blanking out the insults barked at them by their father.

The brute squandered his meager income on the

27

horses, booze, and the lottery.

The family's sad financial situation went from bad to worse, thanks to the money spent on the Sunday as well as the Wednesday drawings.

It was not unusual for the abused woman to talk to herself. Her soliloquies were frequent. Even though her husband was a nonentity, in his presence she became as meek as a lamb. "Damn lottery," she often muttered, "the Sunday drawings are bad enough and now they have this Wednesday one too."

In no time whatsoever the Wednesday drawing was established, on an equal footing with the Sunday one, as a national vice. Now, twice a week, not just once, the town came to halt at midday every Sunday and nowadays every Wednesday too; ears and eyes, with an anxiety frequently bordering on anguish, were riveted on the numbers Lady Luck announces.

When the ceremony in the Santa Ana Plaza was over, curses and sobs filled up the most wretched of the shacks. Every Sunday, every Wednesday. . . .

One Tuesday during the summer the desperate mother of the snotty-nosed brats decided to get two mongrels, the kind that normally go ownerless from birth to death. She had particularly noted how these animals in one way or another manage to find a way to satisfy their daily hunger.

In the poverty-ridden, filthy, nauseous neighborhood, everyone began to gossip about the business of the dogs in the drunkard's home.

"Ohoy! What happen neighbor? How things going?"

"O.K. yes, I struggling along."

"Neighbor, you hear the business about the dogs?"

"Yes man, so is when this business start?"

"Well, in the cry-cry children house. . . ."

"Well look what happen, nuh! They don't have a thing to eat and now they gone and get dog."

28

"Is truth. But that is them business, yes, my dear; now I suppose them is decent high-class people."

Coal and Milk were emaciated, mangy mongrels. In their hovel the little brats constantly played with the dogs, the only toys they ever had. The favorite game was "little doggies." The hungry children pretending to be puppies took turns sucking Milk's udders. Their mother turned a blind eye to the source of her children's happy shouts.

Coal and Milk only went into the streets in the early morning.

The alcoholic as usual got home drunk every other week, his pants soaked in urine. After spending his last cent on the horses, rum, and gambling, he would calmly sit down to the table expecting his wife to feed him. Without a thought as to where the woman got the money for the food, the man would sniff it then lick the three plates clean, thinking that he was eating some *sancocho* or *angú* or *guacho*, or some kind of puree.

He was imbibing more than ever now. He had more money to support his habit, since his wife no longer hassled him for food money, and it was no longer necessary to pilfer his pockets as he slept off his drunk.

Bright and early every morning the hungry children's mother would let out her dogs. Coal and Milk knew the way with their eyes closed and always returned at the usual time.

In Marañon, a down-trodden ghetto, the neighbors intensified their vicious gossip about the dogs.

"Eh eh!"

"How things going?"

"Something fishy going on in . . . house."

"Yes, they have the dogs lock up. And now you don't hear no 'Ayeyayaye you son of . . . , why you don't lick down your . . . !' "

"And now they say the children and them drinking

29

milk. You ever hear more?"

"Ah ha, that is nothing. Hear this one. The crotchety neighbor . . . ."

"That low-down one who does be always talking, talking?"

"That one self, look nuh, she tell me that they even eating meat in the rummie house."

"But he does spend all he money on rum, that's why he always so bad."

"I don't like to mind other people business myself, but, another thing . . . ."

"Hurry up, nuh, my rice burning and my mister. . . ."

"Yes, I know, he does turn beast if you give him burn burn."

"So, tell we!"

"Well, Milk always pregnant, and you ever see any pups?"

"Well, I going yes. I ain't want to hear no more about this business."

Bright and early every morning, Coal and Milk trotted off to the municipal slaughterhouse. There they filled up on the intestines foraged from the garbage cans.

When Coal and Milk returned to the shack, well before the others awoke, the mother of the ragged little brats would force the dogs to vomit so that she could provide food for her family.

NOTES

angú   A dish made of plantain that has been cooked and then pounded in a mortar. In Trinidad it is, "pound plantain."
(Angel Revilla includes the term, *angú*, among his Panamanianisms in, *Panameñismos* (Panama: n.p., 1976, p. 18)

guacho   A dish of very white rice cooked with fowl, beef, or pork (Revilla, p. 55)

sancocho This term is defined in the official dictionary of the Spanish language compiled by the Spanish Royal Academy as: (From the Latin *semicoctus*, half cooked) any half-cooked food. 2. An Americanism used throughout South and Central America to refer to a dish made of meat, cassava, plantain and other ingredients. It is commonly taken as breakfast.
     In Trinidad, the term "sancoch" is used to refer to a similar sort of dish.

The Flour Boy

The entire neighborhood was awakened early, as usual, by the desperate shrieks of the boy who lived in room 33 in San Miguel, that most Panamanian of neighborhoods. It was always the same story there, everyday the same screaming and shouting. It was monotonous, unbearably monotonous. Scolding. Licks. Shrieks. The order of events never varied. Scolding. Licks. Shrieks.

Everyday, everybody in the neighborhood commented on the most strange and unusual question of the boy in number 33. They said that other little boys wet themselves in bed, but to crown it all, the boy in number 33 "befloured" himself in bed.

The goodly mother was tired of scolding her little one, and it pained her to punish her own son with such severity, but the hard-headed boy would not obey. And there is none so deaf, as the saying goes, as he who will not hear. He still "befloured" himself in bed. Other mischievousness could be excused but this business of "beflouring" oneself in bed was the last straw. So, every day, reluctantly, the same threat would be repeated: "If you beflour yourself in bed tomorrow, I'll beat you again."

The boy would listen to the warning with resignation, because he knew that tomorrow, today, and yesterday would be identical.

33

Every night, some kind neighbors, Granny Clara and Auntie Felipa, admonished the boy from room 33, "Boy! for God's sake let sleeping dogs lie. . . ."

The boy was precocious.

At an age when other youths could scarcely babble some meaningless utterances, the boy was driving his mother mad with questions she could not answer: "Mama, why do fish die out of water?" "Mama, why does lightning come out of the sky, and what is lightning?" Mama . . . mama . . . mama . . . .

The idle women neighbors often quoted the saying: "Ask me no questions and I'll tell you no lies." However, the frustrated woman would declare day after day, "The inquisitive child gets no candy." And because of his incessant interrogations, the perspicacious flour boy got to taste few candies indeed.

The mother, with great difficulty, found herself obliged to ignore her son's unsettling inquiries, because she could not respond to them with any certainty. Her own education was deficient. In the third grade she was forced to leave Gil Colunje School, located at that time on the outskirts of Lesseps Park. That was the very same public school where the teachers had told her: "In this school there is no room for people of your class." And they advised her to go to the Republic of Haiti School where the authorities, at their whim and fancy, had the habit of placing certain students.

Gil Colunje School was three narrow little streets away from where the flour boy's mother lived, but the other school was thirteen kilometers from her home, near to the ruins of Old Panama.

The young woman's education was prematurely truncated, because in the third week of the school year at The Republic of Haiti School, she had to give up her place to a fellow student who was a resident of the ward of Rio Abajo, where the public school in question was situated.

The flour boy, every afternoon, would go to the Cinco de Mayo Plaza area to play. One evening around dusk, his attention was drawn to the peculiar behavior of the other boys. He observed with embittered eyes that the band of little boys was happily amusing itself playing blind fowl, *lata,* statue, four corners, *florón, mirón-mirón,* but as soon as he approached them they would reject him with jeers.

The flour boy avoided fights with the little rascals, but not out of cowardice. His mother had taught him at a very tender age to take little account of useless folks. It made no sense using up gunpowder to kill buzzards.

The scene played out every afternoon in Lesseps Park with an abomination. The ill-mannered boys threw mud on the white-painted trunks of the leafy trees; they soiled the park benches with manure; they made fun of the elderly people in the park; they threw stones at the parakeets harboured in the trees, silencing the joyful tumult of the winged singers, and an equal and yellow breasts. Not even the curious squirrels with their timid comings and goings managed to escape the wickedness of the band.

The most vulgar spectacle the flour boy witnessed occurred on the occasion when they snatched away his mother's gift from him. The present was a bouquet of flowers. The demented boys tread and spat on the Espiritu Santo flowers, Panama's national flower.

In the neighborhood, while the gossip-mongering women washed their clothes, dishes, rice, they would speak in whispers about Hannibal the drunk, Susan the whore, and Nelson the homosexual. However, the piece of gossip that circulated with the greatest gusto concerned the business of room 33.

"My Pauly wets his bed."

35

"My Rosey too."

"But you all know who. . ."

"Beflours himself in bed?"

They all gave free reign to an uproarious, vulgar, prolonged guffaw.

In the park, the sagacious observer concluded that the gang's repugnant savagery was induced by some stimulus, and, believing the cause of the frenzies to be color-related, everyday he wore a different colored shirt. However, the horrendous shouts, the obscene words, the looks of profound hatred persisted. It was just as if they were all either sons, or nephews, or godsons of a certain Hannibal Sanchez-Rapine, of maniacal and incestuous countenance.

After a painstaking study of the case, to all appearances inexplicable, the boy from number 33 hit upon the explanation. He discovered why the band behaved so barbarously.

The color of his shirt was not the stimulus for the inhuman behavior, it did not really matter if it were blue, red, chocolate, yellow, green. . .

The boy from number 33 pitied his demented peers and, since he was obstinate in his bent on curing their chronic savagery, every night he would throw a pound of flour on himself. The flour boy was black.

NOTES

lata	A type of hide-and-seek game played by children in Panama and Costa Rica (and probably in other areas as well), in which the object hidden is a can or tin — *lata.*
florón	A type of children's game played in Panama (and probably in other countries as well). The children form a circle to play this game.
mirón-mirón	A children's game similar to *florón.*

The Brothel

At the National Institute of Panama, during the solemn ceremony in which the deliriously euphoric students received their baccalaureate diplomas, the graduates had the custom of passing on to the freshmen a most important secret list of names, full of commentaries on the institution's teachers. The most illustrious surname on the list was that of the teacher of the languages of Plato and Cicero.

The popularity of the young mentor, or, more exactly, of the Graeco-Roman prof as he was affectionately called, could be attributed to the affable affection and interest he showed in his dealings with the students.

The young intellectual was amiable, strong, fair, a man of few words, of refined manners, and impeccable in his dress. He was quite a capable polyglot. Besides, he was famous for his meticulousness in academic affairs. He was thoroughly versed in everything relating to the subjects he taught, and he fulfilled his teaching obligations to the letter of the law.

The saying goes that no priest cares to remember his days as a sacristan, notwithstanding the proverb, in the case of the Graeco-Roman prof it was just the opposite. He did not put on any airs, and it was not below his dignity to rub shoulders with the students. He was outspoken; there was no need to carefully weigh his every word, because he always called a spade a spade.

39

He always said unhesitatingly exactly what was on his mind.

It must be pointed out that he was no wet blanket either. In fact, when appropriate, and with moderation, he enjoyed letting himself go.

He would wind up his daily lessons in grand style by quoting his favorite maxims, such as:

Death makes us all equal.

Do unto others as you would have them do unto you.

It is better to be alone than in bad company.

Courtesy does not detract from valor.

Nothing ventured nothing gained.

He who shelters under a good tree will get good shade.

What's good for the goose is not good for the gander.

Time is money.

Don't put off for tomorrow what you can do today.

A friend in need is a friend indeed.

Don't sign a letter without reading it nor drink water you cannot see.

Besides all this, he would often cite the following lines of Manrique:

Nothing in this life is lasting

The good die as well as the bad

The tragedy of the grave makes us all equal.

It was with great difficulty that the learned teacher managed to secure a position in the famed "eagle's nest." He had to fight tooth and nail in spite of having been the Solomon of his class. As a student he would habitually burn the midnight oil in pursuit of his academic goals.

When the Graeco-Roman prof received his diploma, the flabbergasted audience was witness to the absurdity of his being awarded third place on the honor roll, with the first place going to the undeserving and light-headed niece of the vice-principal.

She was offered countless positions in the capital, and
the cheated student was promised some remote little
post in the provinces of Bocas del Toro, Darién, or
Colón, regions notorious for their backwardness and iso-
lation. At the last minute, however, the classics prof
secured a post in the capital, since the girl who "won"
first place was appointed to a big job in the Ministry of
Education. She was the Minister's goddaughter.

Among those registered for the Greek class which met
at 9:00 a.m., was Sophia, the most intractable character
in the class. The Graeco-Roman prof was fed up to the
teeth with the misanthropically inclined young woman
and her tardiness. She usually and invariably arrived
late to the readings and analyses of the *Illiad* and the
Odyssey. She was always the first to shoot out of the
room like a soul possessed while the teacher's mouth
was still formulating the final sentences of the Greek
translation.

One Tuesday, that expert in the languages of Homer
and Virgil, anticipating Sophia's intention, beat her to
it and with a leap placed himself as an obstacle between
her and the door. When the classroom emptied, the
young woman tried between sobs to explain to the
teacher that her problem was very embarrassing and that
she no longer wanted to continue living in this world
since . . . . At that moment the key to the mystery was
lost forever in the deep, covered over by a sea of tears.
The teacher had noticed that Sophia's pitiless class-
mates relentlessly tortured her with their malicious
looks, scornful snickering, and mordant muttering.

No one paid any close attention to the fact that
the seat frequently occupied by Sophia was now be-
coming dust-covered until there appeared in the evening
papers one rainy day the macabre picture of a mutilated
female body. Sophia was stone cold dead.

Sophia's mentor, in spite of his exceedingly busy

teaching schedule, noticed that no one made any comments about the dead girl. He was surprised, too, by the fact that there was absolutely not the slightest mention made of the funeral and the wake for the deceased. And to whom could one offer condolences, the teacher wondered to himself, a little perturbed, during class as a voice commented on the concept of time as related to Penelope's shroud.

At the teacher's insistence, a collection was made in the Greek class in order to purchase a wreath for the deceased. The educator did not realize how futile his efforts would be until he ended up having to bear almost the entire burden, when he found himself forced to go into his own pocket to come up with more than half the cost of the wreath.

The following garbled message was left one day after class on the teacher's desk: "Not a friend in life, not a witness in death. Begrudging flowers and condolences . . . Susana, Sophia's mother, in Villamor."

On reaching the place indicated in the message, the teacher was astonished to find that Villamor was a brothel. The Graeco-Roman prof felt, as the saying goes, trapped between the devil and the deep blue sea. After a considerable period of vacillation, he decided to take the bull by the horns and go on into the brothel. Inside, the music, or more precisely the cacaphony, emanating from the jukebox mixed with the cigarette smoke and the sad smell of cheap perfume.

The drunks seated at the square tables covered with beer bottles carried on their foolish discussions, screaming at the top of their lungs. Others entertained themselves at the pinball machines. But the great majority chatted with the half-naked whores, who constantly circulated among the men; and from time to time one could hear:

"Let's go."

"How much?"

"Five."

"*Balboas*?"

"No! Dollars!"

In the darkness and confusion of the vulgar smelling brothel, some of the hookers approached him believing that he was a client. He, with refined courtesy, put off the harlots, observing that all the Spanish-American accents were represented.

One of the strumpets, the most obstinate of the whores, accosted the teacher and, placed her right hand between his legs and shouted at him:

"Hey, black man. Hey nigger man, buy me a drink."

"That one just looks on," said the barman following up with a guffaw, "and since he got here he just bought one bottle of *Malta Vigor*."

"*Malta Vigor*!" commented the woman, "but that doesn't have a single drop of alcohol."

"You don't see. If he can't even buy a *Balboa* or a *Panamá,* how you think he'll buy you a drink of *Carta Vieja*?"

"Shit! Haul your ar. . . "

"This one is a real stingy louse."

The teacher tried to get away from the strumpet, following the example of the drunks who, in such straits, would say, I'm coming right back. I'm just going to take a leak," as they set out for the bathroom. But, before he could get away, the slut threw him a disdainful look, and at the same time mumbled, "Shit head. You ain't buy me a drink, and you come asking me for Susana. Look man, don't play the arse. That woman have more man than the army!" The harlot complained that she had not made any tricks since the night before. And she went off grumbling that if Susana's sweetness came with music, hers came with music and real honey, and cost the same to boot.

In a corner of the brothel, a couple was dancing, if what they were doing could be called dancing; the man and the trollop, both drunk, sweaty, and filthy, looked like a two-headed monster in the throes of an epileptic fit.

In another corner of the brothel, the polyglot could observe the buying and selling of dismal joy in that nauseous place that, undoubtedly, not even street mongrels in heat would frequent. After a while a drunk stammered out:

"Come on Susana, let's go."

"Cash!"

"I'll pay you in two weeks."

"Cash on the spot."

"O shit man! You can't give it to me on credit?"

"No money, no love!"

At last Sophia's teacher discovered who Susana was. She was a cross-eyed woman, with a disfigured face marked horribly by an old scar from ear to ear. Besides, her breasts were flabby, fallen, wrinkled. Susana's vaginal frenzy was very popular with the drunks.

When the Graeco-Roman prof tried, money in hand, to explain his intent, his throat got all lumped up. Without listening properly to the teacher's nervous words, Susana the famous prostitute looked dead at him and screamed out coarsely: "You coming by me? You damn nigger: you not in my class. Shit-head nigger man! But look at that, nuh! Go to hell man, you really brave yes. Oh shit man! I don't sleep with no nigger men. No way! Never, never, never! No, no, no, man! Not with no nigger man! Mother of God! Better kill me dead a thousand times." Susana concluded with a badly made sign of the cross.

The raucous guffaw of the throng in the brothel, and especially of the bawds themselves, mingled with the stench of the drunks' urine and vomit.

NOTES

Malta Vigor	The brand name of nonalcoholic malt beverage sold in Panama.
balboa	A Panamanian monetary unit, equal to $1.00U.S. It is also the brand name of a beer sold in Panama.
Carta Vieja	The brand name of a rum sold in Panama.
Panamá	The brand name of a beer sold in Panama.

Honeymoon

Around the turn of the century, thousands of black people from the West Indies left their families and their native soil to emigrate to Panama looking for work, when the North Americans took over control of the construction of the Canal. This latter occurred when it became obvious that the Compagnie Universelle du Canal Interocéanique's undertaking had been a complete flop. The celebrated French engineer, Ferdinand Marie de Lesseps, failed to repeat the Suez feat on the tropical isthmus.

With the wave of West Indians flowing to the shelter of the Panamanian shores, came James Douglin and Lena McZeno, familiarly known as Papa James and Nenen. She hailed from Jamaica, and he from Barbados. If one were to have tallied the combined ages of them both at that time the sum would not have exceeded a score and a quarter.

Once in Panama, the two young island people got to know each other as they slaved on the Culebra excavation, notorious for its frequent cave-ins in the course of the construction of the Panama Canal.

Nenen had to resort to the trick of pretending to be a male so that she could find work at that site with its particularly strenuous tasks.

It was a time when while black folks sweated from sunup to sundown in the implacable tropical climate earning ten cents an hour, illiterate North Americans from Alabama and Georgia, like Mister Boss, were given twenty dollars an hour.

The majority of the North Americans were the black workers' "water boys."

Papa James and Nenen fell in love shortly after they met. And, with the double objective of spending their time off together as well as saving some pennies from their meager wages, they rented a single room in Guachapalí. In that poorest of the poor Panamanian neighborhood with its squalid dwellings full of roaches, rats, and West Indians, the owners of the tenement houses pitilessly exploited the newly arrived black emigrants, who spoke only a few words of bad Spanish.

In spite of the financial hardships faced in their new country, love and goodness flourished in the single room of the West Indian lovers. Without selfishness they shared the enjoyment of their bread with all their neighbors regardless of race or religion. Papa James and Nenen's favorite saying was: "Do good to people, it doesn't matter who they are."

The infants left to expire in the stinking alleyways of the Guachapalí neighborhood found a refuge in the humble home of those two loving black people. Big and small, they were all received there with affectionate and open arms, in spite of Papa James and Nenen being constantly admonished that:

> He who raises another's child
> out of caprice or on a whim
> can take it for sure
> that he will regret it.

They took no notice of the negative advice. They reasoned that foolish talk deserves a deaf ear.

On Sunday evenings, after the lottery drawing, the West Indian couple used to saunter through the streets of Panama City. On one occasion during their Sunday stroll, a shower caught the walkers by surprise between the Cinco de Mayo Plaza and Lesseps Park. Papa James and Nenen hurried home to get out of the rain. Both stopped at a dark alleyway on hearing a little pickney's pitiful cries. The shrieking newborn infant had been placed in a garbage can, wrapped in newspaper, near to a dog in an advanced state of decomposition. Nenen speedily effected the rescue, for the stench of the dog induced violent nausea.

The bundle found by the two black people in that garbage can in the wretched neighborhood had been put there by a servant of Doña Blanca Susana Diana Regina Marta de las Casas Arias Madriz y Arias, a lady of Spanish lineage. Her constant boast was that her aristocratic blood could be traced back to her maternal great-great-grandmother, who was a niece of the famous Count Executioner Inquisitor, the favorite lover of María Luisa, the frivolous Spanish queen. The abandoned child was the fruit of a secret love affair between Doña Blanca Susana, a distinguished Panamanian lady of the highest social circles, and an eminent diplomat plenipotentiary of the Third Reich. The Teutonic emissary was a first cousin of Field Marshal Erich von Manstein, and an intimate friend of General Walter Seyditz-Kurzbach.

The years went by. The child grew up healthy and full of life in the home of the goodly West Indians. In public, people would frequently comment on the anomaly of so blond and graceful a creature in the arms of black folks. On occasions peering eyes cast incredulous looks at the blond lips that hailed Papa James and Nenen as "papa" and "mama."

The sum of the years increased. The new pupil was registered at the Pedro J. Sosa primary school. On the third day of classes Papa James and Nenen found the boy bathed in tears, his nose gushing blood, his hair smeared with manure.

"What happened, Fulo?" asked Papa James, all in a rage.

"They be. . . be. . . beat me. . . me. . . u. . . u. . . p i. . . i. . . n s. . . s. . . s. . . school."

"Who?" shouted Nenen, angered and speaking stridently.

"The o. . . o. . . other ki. . . ki. . . kids."

"And what did the teacher do?" his infuriated guardians inquired in unison.

"No. . . no. . . nothing." babbled the battered boy.

Witnesses of the vulgar incident later declared that at recess time a gang of Fulo's fellow students began to beat up on him because he lived with black people. The teacher gleefully condoned the unfair attack since she, a *chiricana*, was fed up seeing so many *chombos* in Panama. The heartless teacher did not realize that after all is said and done death, as the saying goes, makes us all equal.

During his years at school, in spite of the obstacles posed and the mockery hurled at him by students and teachers, Fulo was an outstanding, untiringly stubborn pupil.

At the National Institute of Panama, a secondary school, Fulo obtained his baccalaureate with honors. In spite of his academic triumph, he never managed to get a scholarship to go to university. Scholarships, as was the custom, were reserved for the sons, nephews and nieces, and godchildren (no matter how thick-headed they were) of the people with influence. No account at all was taken of the fact that the best Salamanca education cannot make up for what nature did not bestow.

To pay for Fulo's university expenses, Papa James looked for a second job as well as other odd jobs on

Saturdays and even Sundays. Nenen also went out to work. She applied herself to washing and ironing neighbors' clothes for a modest fee. Besides this, every night, at the corner of 21st and 3rd of November, she sold *chicheme, bollos, carimañolas*, bakes, souce, pigeon-pea soup, patties, fried fish, escoveitched fish, black pudding, *sancocho*, and *guacho*. She also offered her customers lottery tickets, *chance casado, bolita*, raffle tickets . . . .

The business at times brought some distress, because the clientele, rather roguish for the most part, was tightfisted and always seemed to want everything "on trust."

Papa James and Nenen managed to finance Fulo's studies as well as those of their other adopted children.

The West Indian couple never had any issue of their own. But they adopted an army of children. Those of the first generation were: Henrietta, Myrtle, Marcus, Cleveland, Velia, Claude . . . .

The list of the second generation, offspring of the first, includes: Lito, Mami, Turo, Elsa, Luzmilla, Vicente, Argelis, Anita, Toño . . . .

At the University of Panama, Fulo met Lidis in an English course taught by Professor Gibbs.

Lidis, a beautiful young woman, came from Chiriquí, one of the provinces of Panama. (Some *chiricanos* like to see their province as an independent nation, repulsed by the idea of having to be part of a country that, in their opinion, has too many black inhabitants. Those subscribing to this point of view ignore the most important contributions made by black people to Panama's economy and culture.)

Lidis's father simply could not stand the sight of black people. The gentleman was an influential businessman. He numbered provincial governors and high officials of the oligarchical government among his friends and buddies.

In its early stages the friendship between Fulo and Lidis went very well. The two young university people were inseparable, they got along well together, and people said they were made for each other.

At the university Fulo had an advantage in his English course. He spoke that language sufficiently well, since his first tutors had taught him the phrases and expressions that they themselves had learned as children in their West Indian homes.

Lidis at first would have flunked the language of Shakespeare. But, with the help of Fulo, her intimate friend, little by little her grades improved.

"Uatá," she would say.

"It's 'water,' " he would lovingly correct.

"Uatá mara chu."

"No, no, sweetheart. It is: 'What is the matter with you? ' "

"What is de mara. . . ."

"Almost, almost, darling. Listen. 'What is the. . . .' "

An ominous idyl was blossoming in their young hearts.

Every date brought euphoric enjoyment.

Since Lidis did not know the capital city, Fulo took her on a tour of the ruins of Old Panama, the Paseo de Las Bóvedas, St. Joseph's Church (famous for its Golden Altar), the Panama Canal, the San Blas islands, the Las Perlas archipelago.

During the summer holidays the two lovers pined for each other, because Lidis spent them in David, a city some four hundred and sixty kilometers to the west of the capital, very near to the Costa Rican border.

One Tuesday in summer Fulo decided, after thinking it over carefully, to make a trip to Chiriquí to ask for the hand of his "adorable torment."

His girlfriend's parents were very impressed with the

polished young gentleman and expressed their eagerness to meet their future son-in-law's family. It was arranged that the meeting to make the necessary introductions and to fix the happy date for the wedding would take place in the Lesseps Room, with its eighteenth century decor, at the El Panama Hotel.

Before returning to the capital, the husband-and wife-to-be and the future mother-in-law made a three day trip together to Boquete, Cerro Punta, and Puerto Armuelles in the Valle de la Luna.

When the day finally arrived for the meeting in Panama City between the husband and wife-to-be and their future fathers- and mothers-in-law, Lidis's parents made the trip from David to Panama in their own light aircraft. At the appointed hour, Lidis and her parents nervously awaited the arrival of the absent ones, who got there thirty-three minutes late, because the bus in which they were travelling broke down halfway through the journey, and all the passengers had to look for another bus. The ones who were making their way to the Lesseps Room got into a taxi. But, to crown it all, they had to go first to the St. Thomas Hospital and finally to the National Guard Barracks to file a police report. The taxi in which they were travelling had run over an old woman on the Vía España. The woman's death had been swift and violent. Furthermore, the driver had a heart attack.

When Papa James, Nenen, and Fulo finally reached the El Panama Hotel, Lidis's mother almost fainted to find herself face to face with Nenen.

The bride-to-be's father shouted furiously:

"I don't find this at all funny. I think it's a disgusting joke."

"What did you say," thundered the indignant young man hoarsely and angrily.

"I don't want any monkey grandchildren in the fami-

53

ly." blurted out the *chiricano*.

"But, papa . . . ."

"Be quiet! Let's get out of here. Right now!"

Mother and daughter dared not utter a word; what is more, with tails between their legs, they meekly followed the father, who almost knocked over those present, as he rushed from the room like a soul snatched off by the devil.

The attitude of this wealthy yokel would not have surprised any one who had already had dealings with him. Whenever he alluded to his business associates, he never spoke of Mr. Wong, Mr. Garibaldi, or Mr. Westerman, but the *macaco,* the *bachiche*, the *chombo*. And for the latter he had a whole litany of insults stored up: African shit head, damn West Indian, *yumeca, guari-guari*, nigger, big lip, big nose, *coco liso*, black-pepper hair, *conguito,* monkey, burnt bread, *morolo, meco, rabiprieto* . . . .

Back in Chiriquí Lidis was told, better dead a thousand times . . . .

At dusk one evening, when mother and daughter were alone, the thread of their conversation . . . .

"Mama, there is something I have to clear up."

"Child, don't be stubborn; your father is pig-headed."

"But Fulo is not the child . . . ."

"For God's sake! Please, change the topic. As far as that matter is concerned, it's water under the bridge."

"But, Fulo . . . ."

"Enough, enough. Remember it's best not to rub salt in the wound."

"Please mother, listen."

"I'm not about to . . . besides, your father is the boss here."

"But . . . ."

"Stop it, stop it! Let me give you some sound advice. Always stick to your own kind, and, as for Fulo: no way. I want a white son-in-law, even a white horse will do."

"But . . . ."

"This business of Fulo is harebrained nonsense. Why do you want to blacken the family?"

"But. . . ."

"You knew very well that your father simply cannot stand the sight of blacks. Please, the next time don't start by leaping off the deep end."

The young woman was forbidden the study of English. No sooner said than done. The wealthy family shipped their daughter off to the Sorbonne. There she studied the language of Madame Bovary for many years. Then they moved her to Florence to study the painting, the sculpture, and the music of Tintoretto, Cellini, and Vivaldi.

The years went by with eternal slowness. However, the business of out of sight out of mind did not work for Fulo and Lidis. On the first occasion that they met by pure chance at the Bella Vista Theatre, the gala night of the renowned Bolshoi Ballet Company, the young people talked for hours, until dawn, in a cafe on the Vía España. Afterwards they dated secretly so as to avoid all problems.

The lovers prudently thought over the thorny business of their love affair. They decided that, after all is said and done, they alone had the right to be the masters of their destiny; and they made up their minds to get married even though they would have to fight tooth and nail to win happiness.

On their wedding day, Nenen prepared her famous rice and peas with coconut milk, along with chicken, potato salad . . . .

Everyone ate, drank, and danced, greatly enjoying themselves.

On that festive occasion, the bride's parents were conspiciously absent.

Lidis did not mind not having gotten married in Christ the King Church, with the Archbishop or the Apolostic Nuncio officiating at a nuptial Mass attended by the famous Mr and Mrs So-and-So's of the aristocratic *chiricano* set. Also, it did not seem so vital to her not to have hosted a banquet and formal ball at the exclusive Union Club or at some Canal Zone residence. She reasoned to herself: "It is better to have bread with love than chicken with pain." She was happy with plain honest folk. In such an atmosphere there was no need for airs and masks.

A messenger from the national postal service interrupted the merry party with his announcement:

"Telegram for Miss Lidis."

"Here she is," indicated a guest.

She was so surprised and nervous . . . .

Fulo read:

Congratulations Fulo and Lidis!

With our whole hearts we regret not being with you on this very special moment for you both, but we have not forgotten, never. We will see each other sooner than you can imagine.

I have to take your mummy off to Europe for urgent consultation with various specialists.

We have reserved our light aircraft for you at the Paitilla airport so that you can spend your honeymoon on Buchi Island. There, you will find champagne and a fabulous wedding gift.

Have a good time. Kisses and hugs.

Daddy and Mummy.

They all wept for joy on hearing the loving message from Lidis's parents.

The bride and groom had planned to spend their

honeymoon on the island of Taboga. But, at the last minute, so as not to offend the absent mother- and father-in-law, they decided to accept their wedding gift. However, they did not make use of the light aircraft. The newlyweds thought it more romantic to opt for making the trip in the yacht *Urracá*, Lidis's parents' luxury boat.

With great difficulty the young couple managed to get away from the hugs and kisses of that joyful party. From the Balboa docks they set sail for the bride's parents' island.

When they got to the enchanting island, the delicate moonlight was already casting its reflections on the calm sea, which, with its white foam, caressed Buchí Island, a veritable tropical paradise.

In the island's most elegant cabin, while the bride sipped champagne to cover up her Catholic nervousness, Fulo mused over the suspect and sudden change in attitude of his *chiricano* in-laws. But the romantic tropical music, the gentle sea breeze, the sky crowned with stars inflamed their passion.

"Let's go look for the gift from . . . ."

"But, honey?"

"Later, my love."

"No, no, no!"

"Oh, don't be such a bad boy."

"In the morning, princess. Now . . . ."

Frenzied kisses. Volcanic passion. Two naked bodies entwined.

The tender caresses cooled off when Fulo observed that his wife was on the point of death. He got up. Light. Horror. Fright. Terror.

Lidis's naked, blood-stained body was bright vivid red from head to toe. In the nuptial bed. . . . Eyes. Ears. Fingers. Arms. Legs. The bride's mother's body had been completely cut up into several pieces. Fulo ran to the bathroom to vomit. There he tripped over a body. His father-in-law had hanged himself. On the mirror, written in red makeup was: "A thousand times better dead . . . !"

On the Coiba prison island, Fulo rots away, sentenced to jail for life.

In the sad single room in Guachapalí, the elderly ailing West Indians keep their windows and door hermetically closed. The gaily flowering plants that once adorned the windows have withered up. The great hullabaloo of the *bimbín* birds has been silenced.

All over the Republic, for an entire week, Papa James's and Nenen's photos appeared on the front page of every morning and evening paper in the country. The bold headlines proclaimed: CRIME OF THE CENTURY IN PANAMA. THE SON OF A NEGRO COUPLE POISONS WIFE AFTER MURDERING RICH MOTHER- AND FATHER-IN-LAW ON BUCHI ISLAND.

In Panama, (a nation where more than ninety percent of the population does not read, and if any reading is done it is limited to romantic comics and illustrated novels) everyone, especially the illiterates, in the whorehouses, in bars, in homes, on seeing the photos in the papers commented:

"Well I never! Look what happen! Miss Mary, the killer is some black people son."

"Oh shit! Is true yes Joe man. Yes he's a *chombo*."

"The dead man was a big shot."

"The criminal is a *chombo*."

"Oh shit!

"He's a *chombo*."

"*chombo*."

NOTES

bolita	Any illegal game of chance (Angel Revilla, *Panamenismos*. Panama, 1976, p. 24).
bollo	A food item made from a corn-meal dough, formed into a cylindrical shape, wrapped in plantain leaf, and cooked by boiling.
carimañola	A meat patty made from cassava flour and prepared by frying.
chance casado	Lottery tickets sold only in paired combinations determined by the individual sellers.
chicheme	A hominy porridge.
chiricano	An inhabitant of Chiriquí, a province on Panama's Pacific coast. It and Bocas del Toro are the two provinces contiguous with Costa Rica.
chombo	A term used to refer to Panamanians of Anglophone Caribbean background. It is usually considered insulting.
guacho	A dish of very white rice cooked with poultry, beef, or pork (Revilla, p. 55).
sancocho	This term is defined in the offi-

cial dictionary of the Spanish language compiled by the Spanish Royal Academy as: (From the Latin *semicoctus*, half cooked) any half-cooked food. 2. An Americanism used throughout South and Central America to refer to a dish made of meat, cassava, plantain and other ingredients, which is commonly taken as breakfast.

In Trinidad, the term "sancoch" is used to refer to a similar sort of dish.

The Third Illusion

The termite-ravaged doors of the tailor shop were closed every night at nine o'clock sharp. Nelson María, the neighborhood tailor, on finding himself alone would gaily declare to Josefa, a mannequin: "Now dearie, you and I have a lot to gossip about." The quite detailed make-believe conversation that ensued between tailor and mannequin was about things that are normally the subject matter of women's conversations.

At the usual time, the effeminate man and his female friend dressed up in fine blouses and long skirts, carefully tailored in the shop.

Nelson María was cross-eyed, toothless, and a stutterer. He had the voice, manners, and gestures of a sissy. He was addicted to marijuana, other people's property, and loud argumentation. Besides which, he was a great one for sucking thick caramels.

Nelson María had a first cousin called Hannibal, a chronic drunk. The tailor also had two sisters: Susanna, of questionable reputation, and Diana, the virago of the family.

In Chorrillo, an unhealthy Panamanian neighborhood, the piece of gossip on everyone's lips was the business about Nelson María being a faggot.

"Neighbor, the boys are saying that the tailor is queer."

61

"Nonsense! That's a false rumor."

"Well, you can always tell a lame man, even when he's sitting down."

"You're wrong. Nelson María is very manly, and just look at how he hangs out with those foulmouthed roughnecks."

"That's nothing."

"And in the tailor shop they smoke a lot of grass."

"That's pure foolishness. You know, a good cover hides a whole lot."

Certain incidents that took place in the tailor shop were already giving even the most incredulous neighbors some food for thought. Some clients wondered seriously about the need to be measured three times every time they ordered a pair of trousers. What disgusted the clientele most was the tailor's "accidentally" fondling them all between their legs while taking their measurements.

Every time Nelson María went out to buy material, buttons, needles, a band of little boys would pursue him along Central Avenue, Salsipuedes, and Avenida de los Mártires. A chorus of childish voices would yell obscenities at the tailor. But, whenever he lost his patience, he would shout out: "What I am is my business!"

"Thief."

"But I'm not black."

"Pothead."

"But I'm not black."

"Faggot."

"But I'm not black."

In Chorrillo's doorways, scandalmongers asserted that the tailor's condition was the result of some obeah put on him as a child. In truth and in fact, the matter had nothing to do with obeah. When Nelson María was nine years old, he discovered that the business about the

stork was a fairy tale. He also unmasked the myth of
the Three Wise Men. However, it was the third illusion
that really hurt the boy. Picogrande, the neighborhood
satyr, one summer night, explained to Nelson María,
then a skinny, anemic, rickety boy longing to grow up
brave and strong like the star of the Tarzan movies. . . .

Since that insidious night, in the obscure silence of
the bedroom, in the same bed, night after night, three
naked bodies pet and fondle: Nelson María, Josefa,
and Picogrande.

The Morgue

At the Cristóbal courthouse, on the Panama Canal Zone, when the Indian heard the harsh sentence that clamorously assaulted his eardrums, he declared in an undertone, with fatalistic resignation: "I was born naked, I am naked now, so I have neither lost nor gained."

Throughout the brief trial the only words that the accused would murmur from time to time were: "Just for one lousy horse."

The defense attorney in his eloquent summation tried to persuade the jury that justice would not be served if the victim were punished, and not the guilty party. The intercessor considered the accused a victim of an unjust society. From the beginning of the trial he had kept saying to himself over and over: "It's time now to change this arrogant posture. When a Panamanian steals one *balboa* he is taken off to jail whereas a Zone resident who steals one million is rewarded with a title."

Canal Zone justice condemned the defendant to the chain gang "In perpetuity." They took possession of the poor Indian's body and soul "In perpetuity," just as they had already done with Panama's sovereignty.

The judge, speaking English with a North American accent, ordered the Indian to be taken away as soon as possible to the Gamboa Penitentiary on the Canal Zone.

65

It was to that very same hell that Lester Leon Greaves, an Afro-Panamanian, had been committed, also "In perpetuity," unjustly accused of having raped a Canal Zone whore.

A black man was removed from before the bench with a bloodied head. He had interrupted the sophistic solemnity of the occasion by shouting out right after the sentence was pronounced: "What a hell of a life, one way or another the poor man is sure to get screwed." The Indian's friend was protesting the fact that the cure was worse than the sickness.

The Indians had gotten to Colon City, on the Atlantic side of the Isthmus, after having journeyed on foot for several days, just to be present when justice was meted out by these men with that sinister blue stare. After the sentencing, they marched submissively out of the courtroom in Indian file, silent, defeated, exiled . . . . They went off with heads bowed, just as they have kept them since that hapless day when the Santa María, the Pinta, and the Nina chanced upon Guanahaní.

As the Indians filed out, a pot-bellied curate, stationed by the door, blessed them in monotonous tones after they had all kissed his hand. The priest as a kind of consolation declared: "My children, in heaven you will have . . . ."

* * *

In the emergency room of the Amador Guerrero Hospital, the black man with his head now bandaged raged at the North American magistrate's disrespectful attitude. The black man was especially displeased that the judge should speak to the Indian with such disdain Every time the jurist alluded to the convicted man, he would say: "That Indian." He did not even use the accused's Christian name, and, furthermore, he could not care less whether the accused was Cuna, Chocoe or Guaymi.

* * *

The Indian had come to Colon as a child, originally from a village so forsaken that not even the municipal cartographer had taken note of its existence.

At the age of thirteen, the Indian realized that the same Christian family had bought up in advance a half dozen of his brothers and sisters for less than three *balboas*. He, however, was traded for a sorry nag (a flock of buzzards, birds of prey, pursued him, minute by minute, hovering around in the tropical air in anticipation of an imminent banquet).

Little by little the Indian's rancor intensified.

The Indian's owners, an aristocratic Colon family, considered the boy stupid and useless, because he could not yield as much as three farm oxen.

One day the lad fled from his plantation prison. Since he was unskilled and jobless, he found himself obliged to sleep wherever night found him and to eat the garbage the dogs took out of the stinking trash cans in the sickening alleys.

The Indian managed, at long last, to get a lowly job at the morgue. There, his rancor took on a deviant form.

One night, they caught him red-handed — he habitually had sexual intercourse with the corpses, glassy blue gaze and all.

NOTE

balboa. A Panamanian monetary unit, equal to $1.00 US.

Carnival Tuesday

That carnival Tuesday a frightful cry pierced El Chorrillo's fetid atmosphere. In that neighborhood of indigents it was not uncommon to find bloodstains in the filthy back alleys; stains from cheap blood spilled in the course of those frequent and bitter street brawls: some falling-out among junkies, or some drunken quarrel, or some whores' wrangle.

That Tuesday the tepid blood containing gelatinous globules of tubercular mucus belonged to an innocent young girl. The poor little thing had been dumped in an alleyway in El Chorrillo.

When her mother discovered that the bundle of flesh and bones was once the fruit of her womb, she screamed out to the high heavens. The maddening intensity of her grief all but split her head in two. She drew near and tried to recreate the miracle of Lazarus by dint of her maternal caresses, all in vain. The grief-stricken woman's sobs were shipwrecked in the noisy confusion of King Momo's carnival band as it cavorted through the streets.

* * *

That tragic Tuesday the widow had sent her eldest daughter to work for her because the little ones were

69

sick and filled the wretched shack with their incessant crying.

The widow had worked for a while in Cangrejo. However, she lost her job, for the family in that wealthy suburb was more interested in hiring an Indian woman who had no one in this world, and would be at their beck and call 24 hours a day, 7 days a week, 52 weeks....

In Ancón, on the Canal Zone, it was easy for the widow, with her experience, to find a job as a maid; her mother had been a maid, so too her grandmother, her great grandmother. . . . Besides, on the Canal Zone black women are preferred, being bilingual, industrious, honest. Then, too, there is that strange obsession of the white North American female with having a black nanny.

That Tuesday when the young girl got to the white villa, the lady of the house was not in. Every Tuesday at nine sharp she met with some of her kind at the Clubhouse, just to kill time. Since Canal Zone women were used to always doing exactly as they pleased anyway, they would spend hour after hour, right up to dinner time, swapping gossip, playing canasta, and drinking whisky.

In the kitchen of the white villa, the young girl prepared three dishes of hamburger and French fries along with three glasses of Yankee-Cola for three men guzzling great quantities of Scotch on the patio close to the pool.

The man of the house had taken advantage of his wife's absence to invite over his closest friends. The man of the house was Richard Dixon, president of the social club, The Masked Men of Kalifornia, Kalabama, and Killinois. His buddies were: Edgar Hooper, chief of the Canal Zone police, and John Pitchell, a magistrate of the Balboa court.

All along Central Avenue, the crowd was having a devilishly good time. Just as the revolutionary government had promised, the 1976 carnival was Panama's best ever. All that everyone could talk about was the possible arrival at Tocumen Airport of the Salsa Queen, the fabulous *guaguancó* band, the calypso king. . . .

The streets of the capital were awash with confetti and streamers. Every kind of prejudice was put aside for that day. Blacks, Indians, and Whites rubbed shoulders just as if they were brothers; hand in hand they sang and danced to the sweet *tamborito*, calypso, and salsa tunes. Many Zone residents even joined in the gay revelry, but of course they mistook the *tamborito* for the *cumbia* and kept treading all over the dancers. Besides, they messed up the carnival tunes with their obtrusive: "Excuse me . . . excuse me . . . excuse me. . . ."

In Ancón, the young girl had washed all the clothes, cleaned all the rooms, prepared dinner. . . .

Dixon, Hooper, and Pitchell, muttering obscenities, stripped the little girl, a shower of drivel dropping from their snouts.

The little girl's terrified shrieks mixed indistinguishably with the howls of a bitch cornered in a narrow street. Three dogs mounted the bitch in turn, copulating with unrestrained savagery.

That carnival Tuesday, at the white villa, the little girl thirteen years old. . . .

NOTES

cumbia   A folk dance, and song, manifesting quite significant African influence, that is considered peculiarly Colombian as well as Panamanian.

guaguanco   A so-called Afro-Cuban rhythm.

tamborito   A Panamanian national folk dance that evinces strong African influence.

The Degenerate Woman *

Shortly after the solemn graduation ceremony at the National Institute of Panama, young Obatalá Cubena said goodbye with hugs and kisses to his relatives and colleagues at Tocumen Airport.

Obatalá's trip, a graduation present, was a gift from his good grandparents.

Papa James had already passed away when his grandson received the baccalaureate with honorable mention. The affectionate grandfather had willed a sizeable sum of money for the education of his grandchildren (Papa James managed to save the money thanks to his main job — for forty-four years he had been a contractor-painter for the enterprises of a well-to-do Sephardic family).

The will stipulated that before beginning his university studies Obatalá Cubena was to enjoy the benefits of a trip to Nigeria, Ghana, and Angola.

Nenen's grandson's higher studies were completed with resounding success at Georgetown University, a prestigious Jesuit institution in Washington, D.C., capital of the United States of North America.

After leaving Washington, D.C., the young scholar moved to Cambridge, Massachusetts and obtained his M.D. at the Harvard Medical School.

In a short time the young doctor became a well-

* See page 18 for some discussion of this title.

known virologist, specializing in tropical diseases.

At the Gorgas Hospital laboratories, on Canal Zone, North American and European doctors frequently consulted the learned Afro-Panamanian virologist. One of the most important of Dr. Obatalá Cubena's numerous duties was that of inspecting the clinics and hospitals in the hinterland, in his capacity as Medical Chief of Health Services. Besides, the young physician was responsible for coordinating all the projects of the National Department of Public Health under the aegis of the Ministry of Works, Social Services, and Public Health.

Dr. Obatalá achieved international fame for his knowledge about the terrible Lassa fever.

At the Yale University arbovirus laboratory in New Haven, the Afro Panamanian virologist labored assiduously at the electronic microscope studying the terrible Lassa fever virus. The Center for Disease Control of the United States Public Health Service, with its headquarters in Atlanta, sponsored a trip that enabled Dr. Cubena to continue his research into the African fever at the virology laboratory of the University of Ibadan, Nigeria.

While in Africa, Dr. Obatalá Cubena traveled to Jos, Bassa, and Bauchi. In these three Nigerian towns, the virologist examined Hausa, Fulani, and Margi people. He interested himself above all in the habits of the carrier of the terrible Lassa fever: wild rodents of the species *Mastomys natalensis*.

After the African project, the young virologist moved to the University of California at Los Angeles. There, the city authorities sought the advice of the seasoned expert on the outbreak in the Hispanic community of a disease that was endemic to South America.

In California Dr. Cubena met Genevieve.

Genevieve was an intelligent girl. She loved to contradict others constantly, and, as if this were not enough, she had a fascination for getting into other people's business.

However, some way or another a love affair developed between the unlikely pair.

The first trip the lovers made was to New York, the great North American metropolis. There, they frequented the Metropolitan Opera House to enjoy the performances of *La Bohème, Aida,* and *Carmen*, Dr. Obatalá's favorite operas.

Three weeks later, on their return from the city of skyscrapers, Genevieve invited her exceptionally gifted friend to her parents' home. On that occasion her mother stared disdainfully at the young doctor. She felt an antipathy towards foreigners even though she herself was an immigrant; and her aversion to, and low esteem of, blacks was no secret.

From the very beginning Dr. Obatalá Cubena could read between the lines that Genevieve's uncouth mother had taken a dislike to him.

The unfortunate woman did not even have a high school diploma, nevertheless, she questioned Dr. Cubena's medical knowledge. And, she had the cheek to declare to this cultured gentleman that she had not brought a daughter into the world for any black man....

Even though their love was little by little growing cold, the two young people continued having their interesting chats about Plato, Nietzche, Sartre, or about the works of Dante, Dostoevski, Goethe. On other occasions, the conversation focussed on Beethoven, Mozart, Tchaikovsky. While they talked about philosophy, literature, and music, they listened to the background music of the melodious voices of Mahalia Jackson, Paul Robeson, or Leontyne Price.

As time went on, Dr. Cubena's and Genevieve's dates became less and less frequent.

The globe-trotting virologist, from airport to airport would send postcards to his family and friends in Jamaica, Panama, the United States. . . . The lectures he gave on tropical diseases took him to such far-off capitals as London, Peking, Moscow. . . .

In the summer of 1975, the worn-out doctor decided to catch his breath a little in Europe. Genevieve was beside herself with joy when she received a telegram inviting her to cross the Atlantic.

In Europe, the two travellers admired the treasures of the Prado Museum, the Louvre Palace, the Vatican Palace. . . .

One summer's Tuesday in Cannes, Dr. Obatalá received a telegram entreating his presence in Paris at his earliest convenience in order to diagnose a certain French diplomat's illness. The ambassador had spent some time in Cameroon, Africa.

In the City of Enlightenment, the experts were puzzled by the disease and simply prescribed penicillin with procaine and chloriquine, antimalarial drugs. It was later confirmed that the patient was suffering from the contagious Lassa fever.

While the Afro-Panamanian virologist kept several high officials of the French diplomatic corps under observation, at the invitation of the French authorities, Dr. Cubena and his companion were put up at the Résidence du Bois, one of the most elegant Parisian hotels.

In his leisure moments the eminent physician would invite his girlfriend to go for walks from the Place de la Concorde along the fashionable Champs-Elysées Avenue to the Arc de Triomphe.

One day, it was a Tuesday, from the Eiffel Tower observatory, the two travellers lengthily admired the spectacular Parisian panorama before visiting the nearby Chaillot Palace. Then they took the crowded subway from Trocadero to the Tuileries Gardens. And, after a brief rest, they went, almost running, along Rue de Rivoli, Rue Faubourg St. Honoré, and Boulevard des Capucines to the famous Café de la Paix.

That night they had dinner at Maxim's, and dawn found them at the Moulin Rouge after having been to the Follies Bergères and Le Lido.

On another occasion, they crossed Pont Neuf and marvelled at Notre Dame Cathedral on the Ile de la Cité. On the Rive Gauche, they ambled along Boulevard Saint-Michel up to the Sorbonne as well as the Luxembourg Palace and Gardens.

On Sunday they heard mass at the Sacré-Coeur Basilica. After mass, they bought several paintings at Place du Tertre. There, in an open-air restaurant, they savored a most succulent *boeuf bourgignon* as they watched the inspired artists, brushes and palettes in hand. Their attention was also drawn to the lines of Sunday tourists who flooded the Montmartre.

The conquest of Paris was carried out in several stages, and, as was the case with Tenochtitlan, the conquerors were themselves conquered by the elegance, the charm, the beauty of the capital of the world — Paris.

Dr. Cubena little by little began to notice certain unusual patterns in Genevieve's behavior. She would speak frequently about a friend in Chicago who had been expelled from the convent over some escapade. Besides this, in spite of the tours, she was always depressed. And, from time to time, she would drink to the point of extreme drunkenness. In her sleep she kept mumbling. . . .

Sooner or later Dr. Obatalá Cubena was going to uncover the reason for the secret telephone calls, the feigned indispositions, the clandestine meetings with a certain unidentified person in Burgos, Toledo, Barcelona, and also in Florence, Naples, and Venice.

The virologist noted the strange delight the California woman took in refusing his invitation on three occasions to Versailles, to the Bois de Boulogne and to Colombey-les-deux-Eglises. But the last straw that broke the camel's back was the night when with her coyness and duplicity she tried to make the eminent physician look like a fool during a diplomatic reception at the Elysée Palace. On that occasion Dr. Cubena reflected that apparently bad habits are stronger than good convictions; and furthermore, he reasoned to himself: "Better to be alone than in bad company." That very night he plucked up his courage, and the impudent woman was carted off to the Charles de Gaulle Airport. The doctor with mournful eyes gave her a sad, painful final embrace.

* * *

In Los Angeles, California, a mother is overjoyed that her daughter is no longer trotting off to the ends of the earth with a physician of African origin.

In Genevieve's apartment, every night, she and the mysterious person from Europe bathe themselves in the Bacchic offering. The two bodies, naked, inebriated, burning with erotic passion, caress with volcanic violence, and the two women's tongues on two of those organs that so bewitch men.

The Fireman

Sam Wallace was a special member of the Masked Men of Kalifornia, Kalabama and Killinois. His resounding triumphs in his field of specialization earned him the very popular nickname: Uncle Sam the nigger-killer.

Uncle Sam was a man with a wild white beard. And, in truth, to judge from his speech there could be no doubt that he had a bird's brain in his ox's body.

The nigger-killer was a state-trotter. He had been the guest of honor in the most luxurious hotels of Mississippi, Georgia, New York. . . His suitcase was always packed. The contracts for his services were numerous, and he had to travel from California to Maine to fulfill his nefarious obligations, which he carried out with great attention to detail and with macabre enthusiasm.

Hatred is as powerful as greed. Sam Wallace performed his duties for free.

Uncle Sam fanatically defended the dream of the Masked Men of K.K.K.; everywhere he made it his sacred and patriotic duty to keep everyone of African origin in his or her place.

Since Sam Wallace liked to drink, he frequented bars to be with those of his kind. His favorite topic of conversation was the Mobile affair. The nigger-killer, brimming over with pride, would loudly recount the details of his best contract. However, he would constantly

79

interrupt the thread of his story to complain that he was daily on the lookout for another opportunity like the Mobile one without being able to fulfill his ambitions.

Uncle Sam was so obsessed with his undertakings that now that the Mobile affair could not be repeated his spirits had reached a low ebb. In Mobile, Alabama, Sam Wallace had reduced a black church to rubble.

During the sixties, blacks in the South of the United States justly complained that their existence in that region was worse than that of a cat in a world of dogs. They had been noticing for quite some time that the United States would bare its bayonets in the four corners of the globe in defense of democracy, and that, irony of ironies, North American soldiers of African origin had sacrificed their lives defending the liberty of other peoples when they themselves did not have it in their own country.

The Mobile incident occurred during a hot summer. In Alabama, the governor summoned up bayonets to cut down the aspirations for LIBERTY, EQUALITY, AND FRATERNITY that blacks had been loudly expressing. The children were gathered together in the basement of a church to protect them from the sharpened bayonets, the hard billy sticks, and the ferocious dogs. But, the precautions taken by those black folks were all in vain, for one of Uncle Sam Wallace's sticks of dynamite wreaked a lamentable toll. When the panic and fire had subsided, they found an arm, two legs and three heads in the rubble. It was the three martyred girls — Yoruba, Fanti, and Dahomey — that the black population found hardest to take.

During the burial service for the three girls brutally slain by the explosion, the black folks prayed and, eyes flowing with anguished tears, solemnly sang: "We shall overcome someday. . . ."

In the Whiteonly bar next to the cemetery, Uncle Sam, as guest of honor, was feted with lusty hurrahs for the Yoruba, Fanti, and Dahomey affair.

After the Mobile incident, the eloquent black leader, Martin Luther King, organized people of all races to the shouted response: NO MORE INJUSTICE – NO MORE INJUSTICE – NO MORE INJUSTICE.

* * *

The nigger-killer passionately hated everybody of African origin. He cursed blacks for the Wallace family's impecunious state. Before the Civil War, that southern family had lived in opulence at the expense of their black slaves. However, the post-war Wallace family was obliged for the first time in its history to earn its daily bread by the sweat of its brow. Furthermore, Uncle Sam was particularly incensed, because he considered it the height of insolence that any black person should be so so bold as to reach the point of "demanding" justice. For that reason, Sam Wallace swore a solemn oath to put a stick of dynamite between the legs of every black man. And to . . . every black woman.

* * *

During the United States Bicentenniary, a new contract afforded the nigger-killer the opportunity to travel to Los Angeles, California. A group of North American soldiers of African origin was meeting there for the purpose of bringing to the fore the overlooked exploits of the valiant soldiers of their race. The black soldiers were true veterans. They had all lost an arm or a leg or both in bloody conflicts in Luzon, Seoul, Saigon. . . . On another floor of the same hotel in which the soldiers were lodged, Sam Wallace was preparing a powerful bomb for the occasion. However, the night before, the nigger-killer had gotten totally drunk, and, since his hands were trembling, one of the wires of the bomb was badly connected, causing a premature explosion three hours before the time indicated on the clock of the device. Part of the hotel collapsed and a huge fire engulfed the establishment.

The first fireman to arrive on the scene of the disaster risked his life to save Sam Wallace from the walls that were on the point of caving in on him. In the accident, Uncle Sam lost his sight, his arms and his legs. His charred body slowly disintegrated as he lay dying in bed.

The dying man with great difficulty conveyed to the nurses that, as a last request, he wanted to kiss the hands of the person who had risked his life for him.

The hero was an intrepid fireman. He was of a line of exceedingly heroic soldiers who had fought with valor at Bunker Hill, Vicksburg, in Guam, Germany, Korea, Viet Nam. . . .

The valiant fireman was of African origin.

The Party

Cubena had spent the entire day touching up the final pages of his autobiographical novel — *CHOMBO*. The young writer was besides himself with joy now that he was going at long last to enter a work of his in Panama's prestigious Ricardo Miró Annual Literary Contest.

That summer's evening in Los Angeles, California, the author of the novel, which highlights the hardships of the Afro-Antillean in Panama, had planned to reread for the third time that year the immortal work which begins as follows: "Somewhere in La Mancha, the exact name and place I do not care to recall, there lived, not long ago, a gentleman. . . ." Shortly after he had begun to read the chapter in which the shepherdess Marcela's tale reaches a conclusion, the telephone rang.

"Hello."

"It's Maude."

"How are things?"

"O.K."

"So glad to hear . . . ."

"Want to go to a party?"

"A party?"

"Here at my apartment."

"But . . . ."

"No but's. Some old pals came in and . . . ."

"O.K., I'm a little exhausted but . . . . I'll be

there."

"Great!"

The moon was already high on the horizon when Cubena reached the place of the festivities. The newly arrived guest was received with weak hugs and lukewarm greetings by those present. Maude's friends were a strange lot. They were all dressed up in yellow. Furthermore, the men wore yellow caps, and the women likewise wore yellow bonnets over their yellow wigs. From time to time they saluted each other by making three circles over their foreheads with their index fingers and shouting out: APOLLO, APOLLO, CHIMBOMBA, CHIM BOM BA! APOLLO, APOLLO! RA, RA, RA! APOLLO, APOLLO, APOLLO . . . !

The hostess tried politely to ignore these goings-on, but after all, in the land of the blind — as the saying goes — the one-eyed woman is queen.

The partygoers compared, in an accent that was faintly Dutch, the hours they had chalked up taking sun baths. Since the sun had already retreated behind the Santa Monica mountains, they deplored the fact that the party had to be moved indoors from the apartment pool. There, they danced awkwardly to the beat of the zamba, a hot Afro-Brazilian rhythm. Those who were not dancing, or more precisely those who were not stamping around, were babbling some kind of nonsense. On the whole the thread of conversation centered on their tastes for Dracula, Tarzan or Hitler. However, they all got indignant when Cubena suggested that they try to determine who invented the telephone, the television, the aeroplane, etc. To judge from the replies, it was evident that they had never heard of Alexander G. Bell, John L. Baird, Wilbur and Orville Wright. . . .

Cubena realized that at this party those who knew the least swaggered the most. The pompous folk argued long and loud that Dante, Goethe, and Dostoevski were

84

pianists, and that Rubinstein, Horowith, and Rachman-inoff were novelists. As if this were not enough, they put on great airs roundly denying that Rodin, Carpeaux, and Duchamp-Villon were French sculptors. Trying to exclude Cubena from the conversation, Maude's pals whispered in French, Italian, and Portuguese. But the exasperation of these buffoons welled up past the point of overflowing because the Afro-Panamanian mastered nine languages.

As the night advanced the crowd intensified its strange prancing about and its hair-raising shouts, which had begun as the sun disappeared on the mountain-framed horizon.

In that atmosphere the envious, hostile, hateful stares which they fixed on his dark skin made Cubena feel uncomfortable. Then they all stripped. They smeared each other with a certain yellowish salve, and, in chorus, they implored the birth of a new sun. The strange madness was cured when the first rays of dawn lit up the firmament. However, all this was repeated every night when Cleo, Callipe and Thalia invited Apollo to the Olympian couch.

They were all victims of the "sun tan syndrome."

The African Grannie

That sultry night, the newspaper boys, like the waters of a swollen river, flooded Panama City's maze of streets. The ragged boys, newspapers in hand, loudly cried out: EXTRA. EXTRA. BLACK FEMALE CRIMINAL. EXTRA. BLACK WOMAN. EXTRA. EXTRA. CRIMINAL. EXTRA.

On the following day, the morning papers were bought up as soon as they left the presses. The bold headlines on the front page read: BLACK WOMAN MURDERS EMINENT PANAMANIAN SURGEON.

In the government offices, in the banks, in the brothels, people heatedly discussed the infamous, horrible, ignominious crime.

"You read about the black woman?"

"God Himself could not pardon such a crime."

"I hope they put that black woman behind bars for the rest of her life."

"What life imprisonment!"

"They should set up a firing squad for her right in the middle of Santa Ana Plaza."

"Damn right!"

The black woman in question was an elderly person of ninety-three years.

The murdered surgeon was the grandchild of the black woman's first master.

The accused woman had passed from master to master like any other inherited object in that wealthy, aristocratic, isthmian family. For nine decades the black woman had been nursemaid, cleaner, cook . . .

In jail, the culprit was concerned over the fact that she was devoid of any funds to defray the costs of her defense. All her life her only pay had been her food and lodging.

The accused had no known family. In her youth she had had a daughter, but, a few hours after the birth, they had forced the mother to give away her infant because it would have been a hindrance on her job. And, besides, they had pointed out to her that it would be most important for her to give all her affection to her masters' nieces and nephews.

In Colon City, a young woman lawyer who had never known her grannie became interested in the forthcoming trial, which had already turned into Panama's hot after-dinner conversation piece.

The novice lawyer offered her services free of charge to the elderly black woman. She had little courtroom experience. This was due in large measure to the limited confidence people reposed in her expertise as a female lawyer (at law school a certain professor made her life impossible; he never allowed her to do any practice trials because the little runt of a fellow felt that women had no business being in school, and much more so if they were black.)

Three long years passed.

Finally, on the day the accused's trial began, the defense lawyer realized that the trial judge was the dead man's uncle. Furthermore, the members of the jury were cousins, nephews and nieces, and godchildren of the deceased. As if this were not enough, the old lady claimed total ignorance of certain anomalies that the defense attorney had uncovered in the course of the complicated murder investigation.

From the beginning to the end of the trial the courtroom of the Superior Court filled up to capacity. Spec-
tators from every province in the republic came to the
capital to find out the facts about the most sensational
trial in the Isthmus' history.

All teaching and commercial activity came to a halt
during the trial. In homes all eyes were glued to television sets; in the streets, the passersby listened to a word-
by-word account of the proceedings on their portable
radios.

In the courtroom, while the expert prosecutor, the
victim's godfather, with moving words, delivered his
eloquent final address on the facts of the case, the accused woman's defender listened nervously to her courtroom adversary. From time to time she became en-
grossed in a dream that she had had.

(On the London Wilson family's sugar plantation in
Jamaica, the black slaves labored without rest from sunup to sundown, from the rooster's first cry till the spent
sun went down behind the sea on the horizon.

One evening, at twilight, an *erubinrin* [female slave]
gave birth to an *omobinrin* [daughter] in the canefield
and hid the newborn infant in the dried stalks a little
before the overseer called a halt to the cane cutting.

The slave woman did not want them to sell her pickney as they had done with her other little ones, and
above all she did not want her little girl to become an
erubinrin [slave].

Gazing at the night sky from her tropical hiding place
in company with the *iwe* [frogs] the little girl could see
the Southern Cross constellation.

Every night the buzz of the *yanmumamu* [mosqui-
toes] produced the desired soporific effect on the little
girl.)

"Distinguished ladies and gentlemen of the jury.
There can be no doubt that one of Panama's most

89

talented sons has been brutally cut down. This was a cold-blooded murder."

(The slaves were given much work and little food. The good *iya* [mother] did not eat her portion of food so that she could feed her little daughter.

The undernourished *erubinrin* would frequently fall in a faint in the canefield. Her owner would order the sturdiest *okonrin* [man] in the group to inflict three hundred and thirty-three lashes on the poor *abo* [woman] for her laziness every time she fainted.

She, from time to time, would call upon Obatala, Yango, and Ogun to give her the strength to carry out her secret plan.)

"The illustrious surgeon whose tragic demise is mourned in every corner of our beloved land, distinguished ladies and gentlemen of the jury, was just thirty-three years old. He was in the prime of life. Yes, I repeat, just thirty-three years. Just thirty-three years. And do not forget his contribution to international medicine. Most distinguished members of the jury, thirty-three years old and his reputation was already international. His grandfather was one of our great national heroes."

(The mother protected her offspring with all the strength of her being. Whenever the owner approached on his horse, she would shout: *"Dake, dake, dake"* [Silence]. But when the *omobinrin* [daughter], fastened to her mother's back and covered with a cloth, cried continuously because of the suffocating heat, the *iya* [mother] would sing:

Erin, pa ti ori ogá
Kiniun, pa ti owó ogá
aja, pa ti epón ogá
trala la la la
oíbó buburu
oíbó nika

oíbó omugo
trala la la la
[Elephant, I give you the master's head.
Lion, I give you the master's hand.
Dog, I give you the master's testicles.
Trala la la la
Bad white man
Cruel white man
Stupid white man
Trala la la la]
The owner would go off laughing, his jaws flapping, thinking that his euphoric slave woman must have been singing so beautiful a song to give expression to her felicity.)

"I ask for justice. Most distinguished ladies and gentlemen of the jury. I ask for justice. Three generations of this bereaved, patriotic, Panamanian family sheltered that black woman. Love. Dignity. A roof. Dignity. Food. Dignity. If it were not for the goodness of this illustrious family that black woman . . . I ASK FOR JUSTICE.

(One dark, moonless night, the *iya* [mother] sacrificed a snake, a fish, and a chicken. She offered the *eje* [blood] to her three favorite Yoruba goddesses.

The mother put her *omobinrin* [daughter] into the Great River near Catadupa so that the current would carry her off to Montego Bay.

The little sailor was well wrapped up in a basket and provided with a good supply of *akara* [bread], *wara* [milk] and *oro yinbo* [mangoes].

Every night the magnanimous mother offered sacrifices to Odudua, Oshun and Yemaya asking them to protect her little one on her voyage to freedom.

The little girl who was sent down the *odo* [river] worked at various domestic tasks during her adolescent years. She traveled to Santiago, Cuba, as well as to

91

Miami, New Orleans, New York, and finally she moved to Panama to work on the construction of the Panama Railroad during the period when gold was discovered in California.)

"Most distinguished ladies and gentlemen of the jury. Our beloved country has become even more bereaved. I have just been informed that the murdered man's wife, a most cultured lady, at this most tragic moment for her, grieving over the death of the person she most loved — ladies and gentlemen of the jury — it is deeply distressing for me to have to inform you that the afflicted lady has just had an unfortunate miscarriage. Mother and child, at this very moment, are stone cold dead. The infant who has thus been deprived of happiness and good fortune — ladies and gentlemen of the jury — is a great grandchild of one of the nation's great heroes."

(The rebellious slave woman's fame spread throughout all the islands of the West Indies, and even to the mainland. She helped three hundred and thirty-three slaves escape, she set fire to thirty-three important sugarcane plantations, and instigated three important rebellions in Jamaica. It is said that she was the one who prepared the deadly purgative for making the master's slave concubines abort.)

"This jury has a sacred mission. The death of so illustrious a son of Panama . . . his beautiful wife . . . his child . . .

(The *erubinrin* [slave woman] in Jamaica was never forgotten. As soon as the daughter managed to save some money, she returned to the West Indian island to purchase her *iya*'s [mother's] freedom.

The elderly slave woman had been ailing for a long time, the result of the brutal whippings she had received; and in addition, she was now deaf and blind, the result of a severe blow to the head she had received for not revealing the whereabouts of her *omobinrin* [daughter].

When the ex-slave reached her daughter's home, her cheerful granddaughter, full of happiness, of delirious euphoria, rushed up to embrace her, crying out:

African grannie
don't you recognize me?
I speak like a Spaniard
I pray like a Christian
I sing like an Italian
African grannie
Why don't you recognize me?

The ex-*ilota* died on her third day as a free *abo* [woman].

The little granddaughter, too young to understand what death was, burst into tears thinking that her grannie had gone away so as not to have to answer the question – "African grannie, why don't you recognize me?")

"JUSTICE. JUSTICE. JUSTICE. Distinguished members of the jury – FIAT JUSTICIA, RUAT COELUM. That is all I have to say."

The efforts of the defense went for naught.

With the expected guilty verdict, the elderly black woman was sentenced to three life terms of ninety-nine years each.

The reprobate carried to her grave the secret she had so zealously guarded during her lifetime. The aristocratic mistress had been a foulmouthed drunk and a pothead. She played the prim and proper lady in front of her husband. But the longevous servant had been aware of the fact that her mistress was a goodie-goodie by day and a runabout by night. What is more, every Tuesday the lady would invite the garbage man of that fashionable district of the capital into her bed.

The adulterous woman was the one who, by her own hand, had murdered her spouse shortly after a violent argument over her pregnancy.

The surgeon was a homosexual, impotent, sterile. . . .

The Family

That Tuesday, the man of the house did not get up from the only bed in the room. He slept with legs sprawled. He snored resoundingly.

The tropical midday sun was already heating up the neighborhood's perennial putrid odors.

The woman of the house, the children too, from a very early hour had begun their nervous comings and goings, like ants, in that room in tenement building number thirty-three located in Marañon.

"Please, man, don't be a good-for-nothing! Look for some work, your children are dying of hunger," the angry wife grumbled at point-blank range.

"I'm feeling very sick," was all that came out of the languid-eyed husband's starving lips.

"Don't be so worthless. The early bird catches the worm!"

"O.K., O.K., woman, leave me alone!"

"The boat that's moored doesn't get the cargo."

"Dammit! I told you already, leave me alone! Leave me alone!"

"A dog on his haunches can't chase deer."

"Shit! Stop that crap! Leave me alone! Leave me alone!"

The man was tall and thin. He had harsh, calloused, misshapen hands. From the very day he first learned to scrawl his surname, he had begun to earn his livelihood

95

as best he could as a carpenter, plumber, gardener . . . .

The husband pretended to be indisposed and played dumb that Tuesday, because he did not know how to explain to his wife that he had no shoes. For years now he had been tramping the city streets, up and down, in search of employment. His shoes had left their mark all along Balboa Avenue, Central Avenue, the Vía España... from pillar to post. It was the same for all the main thoroughfares in the Panama Canal Zone.

The barefoot man's spirit was completely broken. Life's harsh blows had given him no respite. At the business establishments where he tried to get a job so as to earn his livelihood, he was rudely and loudly told, "We don't want blacks here." At other places, they would spit out at him a disdainful, "There's no work for people of your kind. . . . Get out of here, big-lipped nigger!" The insulted man would walk away in silence, indignant, irate, thinking that when a black man is down and out, even the dogs urinate on him.

In the bare, dismal room in that very poor neighborhood, there lived six malnourished, painfully rickety, and very frail children — Yoruba, Fanti, Ashanti, Bantu, Congo, and Dahomey. The little ones looked like death warmed over, and all over their arms and legs there were sores full of pus that harbored worms.

Their dwelling looked like a racial showcase. The little ones, in spite of being the offspring of the same parents, were born with grey, green, and blue eyes; nappy, Indian, and straight hair; black, mulatto, and albino skin. From the children's physiognomy, it was clear that their African great grandmothers, black slave women, had been debased, dishonored, bestially violated by European lust.

In the gloomy hovel, its walls of faded colors, the asphyxiating atmosphere was impregnated with the odor of old clothes (all the clothes the family possessed had

been bought in Salsipuedes). The squeaky door generally remained closed.

The home's only window, being always half-shut, pre-
vented the sunlight from flooding the room. The wood-
en floor squealed tearfully under the comings and goings
of the bony inhabitants. In one corner there was a pile
of odds and ends, in another, a coal pot. And, in yet
another there was a humble altar with statues of the
Black Christ of Portobelo, St. Martin de Porres, the
Virgin of Carmen, a Yango talisman, a glass of water,
and three red votive candles.

The Power and Light Company had, some time ago
now, discontinued their electricity service, and for that
reason the hovel had a sepulchral appearance at night.
The flickering flame of three white candles timidly lit
the corners just as at a wake, and the sad sleeping children looked like corpses strewn about on a battlefield
after a fierce conflict.

The only thing there was plenty of in that somber
household was water. Water. With clockwork precision,
every minute, one or two and at times three of the six
children at the same time pitifully implored in unison in
their usual garbled voices: "Mama, I'm hungry. I want
some food." The exasperated mother quickly lost her
patience and almost instinctively shared out blows with
an old broomstick, threatening to give a more thorough
thrashing to those who did not lie down and go to sleep.

"But mama, I'm not sleepy, I'm hungry," blurted out
Congo, the stubbornest one, that Tuesday.

"Mama, sleep can't take away my hunger now," wept
Fanti bitterly, without restraint.

"But, mammy, I don't want any more lie down and
sleep. I want food," babbled Dahomey, the smallest,
weeping for all she was worth.

"Dammit! Everybody go to sleep!" screamed the
mother in a rage, pointing to a corner with a Napoleonic

gesture. The floor that served as a bed was covered with newspapers.

Tears. Hunger. Blows. Hunger. Misery. Hunger. All this was exasperating the barefoot man beyond endurance. Deeply pained, the frustrated man could find no way of remedying his impecunious state. He decided that it was impossible to spend a single second more in that . . . it was imperative that he escape as soon as possible. He looked for his delapidated shoes and with a piece of newspaper he stopped up. . . . He moved hurriedly. He left in a flash. He went out into the street like the Chepano people. He walked around that wretched day, hour after hour, like a somnambulist, like a boat without compass nor rudder, until he wandered off into infinity. . . .

* * *

The woman of the house, with aching bones, always had a tub full of water, just in case a little work came her way. Around the neighborhood, she had a meager clientele, whose washing she sought out at ten cents a load. It was a poorly paid business.

Her profits were minimal, and the clothes were generally so grimy that the poor washerwoman found herself having to sweat blood for a few measly cents. The only thing that kept her going was her favorite proverb: "There is no misfortune that lasts for one hundred years, nor human body that can endure it."

The barefoot man's wife had worked for a short while at the mansion of a well-to-do family in the pompous Bella Vista section. At her job she was entrusted with walking the dogs three times a day, after each meal. But by the third week she was fired from the job, and because of the harmful references she was unable to obtain another position. Her Bella Vista employers accused her of abusing their trust and of a lack of responsibility. According to them she had the audacity to take the high pedigree dogs to empty their bowels in Marañon, her disgusting ghetto infested with roaches and rats, and worse yet she took advantage of the opportunity to look after and feed with dog food her weak, sickly, half-dead children.

Three years had passed, three long, slow, steady, protracted years, since they last saw the provider of the home. The exhausted mother, her face emaciated, her body bent, prematurely aged, while her children took their siesta, thought long and hard beside the cold coal pot on the fact that some people are born stars while others see stars. Her ancestors had been brutally uprooted from Africa to pacify, build, and sow this ungrateful region of America, and now the grandchildren of those same black people who built this nation with their freely given buckets of sweat were barred from sharing in the wealth that they had bequeathed, because Yoruba's, Fanti's, Ashanti's, Bantu's, Congo's, and Dahomey's color was offensive. It was ironic — she thought — that since the days of Adam, one man heats the oven while another eats up the bread. But she consoled herself with the reflection that God chastens but does not destroy, willing herself to accept it by dint of frequently repeating it to herself.

One evening at dusk, when her hurt was hammering pitilessly at the desperate woman, she went to Río Abajo to consult a soothsayer. But her problems were so thorny that she was advised to see the famous Cuban obeah woman from the Juan Díaz area. There she had to sacrifice three white doves, suck the blood from the heart of each one, and take a special bath in urine mixed with yellow nance skins, green mango-tree leaves, black fowl feathers, wild-boar fangs, dog hairs, iguana eggs. . . .

The obeah turned out to be ineffective.

One suffocatingly hot summer afternoon when Yoruba, the eldest daughter, awoke from the usual imposed siesta, her mother sent her to the pharmacy with the last few cents she possessed to buy rat poison. Yoruba reflected on the irony of the situation: the rats about to die from having their fill, and they, from starvation.

The exuberant tropical climate had prematurely awakened the nipples of the young girl, who was only just about to celebrate her ninth birthday. At that tender age her body had already been fondled by the libidinous paws of sprightly old satyres, who promised her money for candy. Yoruba understood the sad situation but said nothing, and instead of buying junk at the artful Chinaman's store, she would buy stale bread, a lot of it, for her little brothers and sisters. Milk, rice, and meat cost an arm and a leg. She had come to realize that eating well in her home meant eating hard bread, complemented by their faithful companion — water. They never lacked for water in that hapless home. Never.

The mother was very devout. The children were obliged to hear Mass every Sunday and holy day at the St. Vincent de Paul church located close to the Gil Colunje school. At meal times, they would always bless the desolate table, three times a day, even though, as was frequently the case, the banquet consisted of simply a rusty little can or a gourd half-filled with water for each members of the family.

The worn-out woman frequently remarked to herself that God should have been more compassionate. She thought that perhaps the Almighty was very busy or was a loafer, and so after careful consideration she decided to help out the All-Powerful. After all, she kept telling herself, it was not just that her children should suffer the consequences of such heartless racial injustice. Be-

sides, it was a real indignity for the descendants of so
noble a line — Pharaoh Taharqa, King Sundiata Keita,
King Tutankhamen — to cohabit with the scum who
people the New World. But repatriation was not possible, since the tentacles of Europe's demented, atro-
cious, implacable hatred had already expanded over the
whole of Africa. After all, it was a better thing to unite
oneself with Olodumare and the other cheerful ancestors in the Kingdom of the Dead.

One afternoon she ordered the children to dress up in
their Sunday rags.

While the sun was going down on the tropical horizon,
she took the dose of poison. As the lethal venom coursed
through the labyrinth of her veins, slowly carrying out
its fatal mission, the mother had sufficient time with
considerable effort to drown her six offsprings in the
perennially full tub of water. She drowned them all —
Yoruba, Fanti, Ashanti, Bantu, Congo, and Dahomey —
one by one, from the biggest to the smallest, with the
anguish of childbirth. Solemnly.

That very night, near to the Paseo de Las Bóvedas,
Hannibal Sánchez-Rapiña, an illiterate, demented loud-
mouth, after having overindulged in Herrerano, Carta
Vieja, and Panama, was as drunk as a lord. Among his
kind, the street people, he was well-known for his attitude and his comments about not being able to stand
the sight of black people. He was fanatically dedicated
to that Panamanianizing mania which proclaimed the
doctrine that after black folks had built the Panamanian
railroad and canal, they ought all to have been deported
from the isthmus, notwithstanding the black West
Indians' important contribution to Panama's economy
and culture.

Hannibal the drunken lout, with his disfigured face
(a horrible scar marked his face from ear to ear), his
macabre smile, his maniacal and incestuous look, and

to boot his cross-eyes, inspired terror. He had murdered a black man who sold lottery tickets and a black woman who hawked her bakes, *bollos, carimañolas*, patties, pork skins, fish, black pudding, turtle eggs . . . . The sharp cold machete had made the heads of the two black folks roll onto the ground, splattering with red stains the sandals of the rustic patrons in the noisy bar, "El Buchí."

Husband and wife together used to frequent the President Remón Hippodrome, the Santa Ana Plaza, the Cockfighters Club, the bars, the brothels, and other public places, selling their merchandise so as to be able to feed, cloth, and educate their offsprings.

* * *

On the third from the last page of the morning papers one Tuesday, the first of April, there appeared the following bold headline: MORE BLACKS DIE, THIS TIME AT HOME AND NOT IN A BARROOM BRAWL.

NOTES

bollo	A food item made from a cornmeal dough, formed into a cylindrical shape, wrapped in plantain leaf, and cooked by boiling.
carimañola	A meat patty made from cassava flour and prepared by frying.
Carta Vieja	The brand name of a rum sold in Panama.
Herrerano	The brand name of an alcoholic beverage sold in Panama.
Panamá	The brand name of an alcoholic beverage sold in Panama.